WHERE'S the DINOSAUR?

1 3 5 7 9 10 8 6 4 2

Published in 2020 by Pop Press,
an imprint of Ebury Publishing,
20 Vauxhall Bridge Road,
London, SW1V 2SA

Pop Press is part of the Penguin Random House
group of companies whose addresses can be
found at global.penguinrandomhouse.com

Penguin
Random House
UK

Copyright © Pop Press 2020
Illustrations: Gergely Fórizs
Copy-Artists: Greta Schönberg,
Martyn Cain and Szilvia Szakall
Design: seagulls.net

www.penguin.co.uk

A CIP catalogue record for this book is
available from the British Library

ISBN: 9781529106985

Colour origination by BORN Ltd
Printed and bound in China

Penguin Random House is committed to a
sustainable future for our business, our readers
and our planet. This book is made from Forest
Stewardship Council® certified paper.

MIX
Paper from
responsible sources
FSC® C018179
www.fsc.org

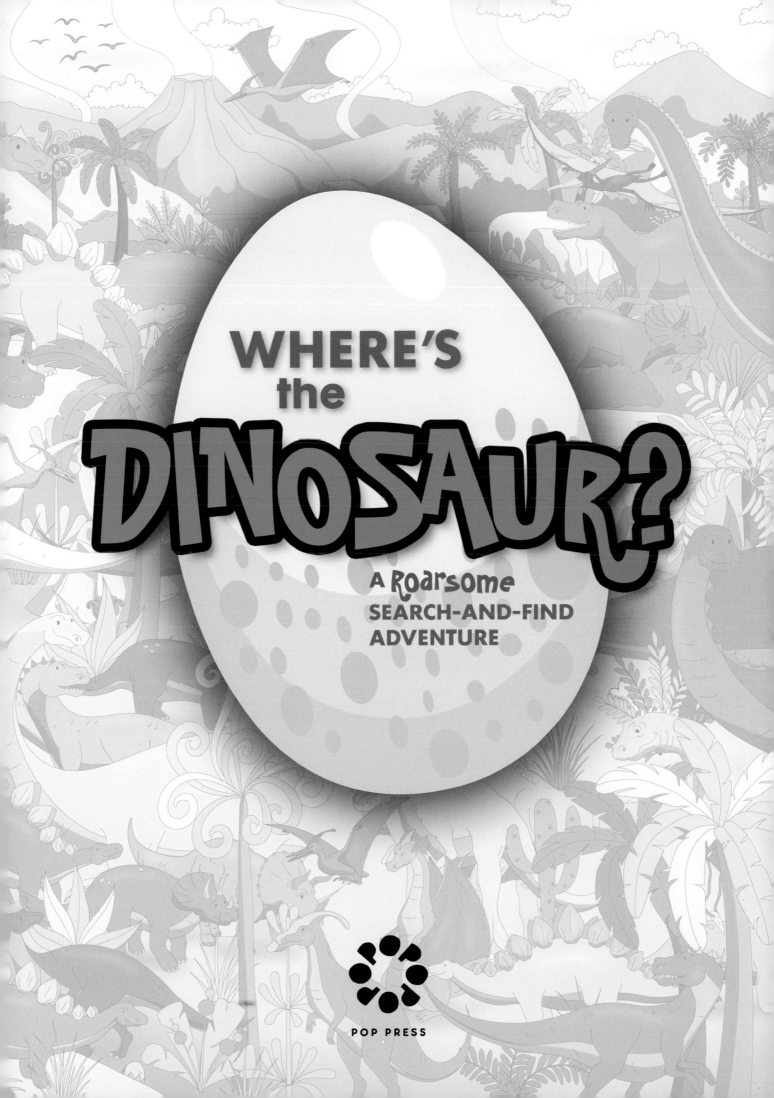

WHERE'S the DINOSAUR?

A Roarsome
SEARCH-AND-FIND
ADVENTURE

POP PRESS

INTRODUCTION

Meet eight time-travelling dinosaurs: Rex, Terry, Rufus, Steggy, Donny, Sarah, Anky and Dippy.

Follow them on their big adventure as they explore the modern world – from the tops of snowy mountains to the depths of the sea and everywhere in between!

Find all eight and their most prized possessions in each scene as they mingle and get lost amongst the crowds.

Their hiding places and a few extra things can be found at the back of the book.

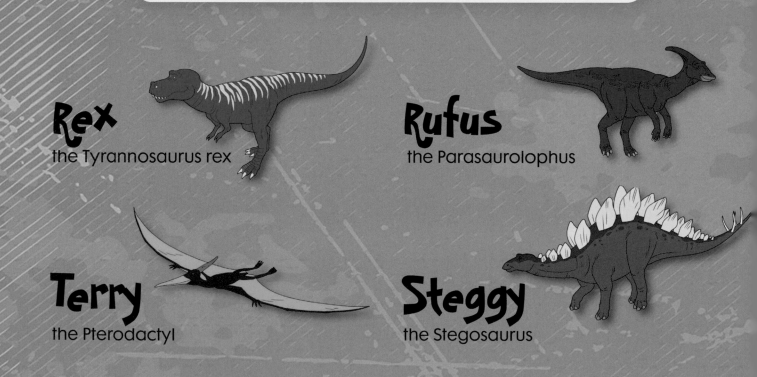

Rex
the Tyrannosaurus rex

Rufus
the Parasaurolophus

Terry
the Pterodactyl

Steggy
the Stegosaurus

FAVOURITE THINGS

Rex, Terry and Rufus each own a collectible dino-egg: Rex has the spotty one, Terry the zig-zag one and Rufus has one with a pink band around it.

Steggy's most prized possession is the beautiful unicorn horn, whilst Donny simply adores the scent of this special flower.

Sarah's favourite is her dino-tooth necklace – she hates to be without it – and Anky likes to curl up tight in his old nest at night. Dippy really loves his toy bone and likes carrying it around.

Help reunite the dinosaurs with their favourite things and find them all in each scene.

Donny
the Iguanodon

Anky
the Ankylosaurus

Sarah
the Triceratops

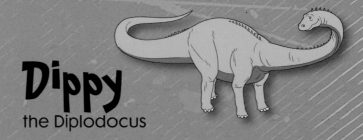

Dippy
the Diplodocus

And so the story begins...

One scorching hot afternoon on
Planet Earth 140 million years ago, in a
place called Prehistoria, eight
cheeky dinosaurs were up to no good.

After spending the morning showing off their
favourite posessions at dino-show-and-tell,
they'd become bored and restless.

Completely disregarding all warnings
to avoid the swirling vortex beyond the
volcanoes, temptation and a passion for
adventure got the better of them...

The dinosaurs (along with their favourite things) tumbled head-over-tail into space! Their crazy journey through the vortex had caused them to shrink dramatically in size.

They weren't alone; it was actually rather busy but the dinosaurs managed to catch a rocket heading to Planet Earth (just not as they knew it)...

This Planet Earth was much busier than their home in Prehistoria, with lots of bright colours, new sounds and smells. This was the 21st Century!

A bit overwhelmed, they spotted a place full of friendly faces so they headed in.

The gang spotted lots of Homo sapiens running in the same direction – very strange. They thought it looked quite fun so they joined in.

The dinosaurs are invited to make an appearance at a very special music festival.

It's time for them to appear on stage but they're busy getting their groove on and are lost amongst the crowd.

They really love crowds of Homo sapiens. Luckily the carnivores have lost their appetite for meat in this strange new world. Look! A football match has just started.

Brr it's chilly here. The dinosaurs worry they've stumbled into the Ice Age. There's lots of powdery snow to play in and a great view from the top of the mountain.

Ice skating is very tricky for dinosaurs! They have to try very hard not to knock everyone over – luckily they can use their tails to balance.

Time to get away from all this cold weather!

The dinosaurs don't manage to get regular tickets but there's still plenty of room in the hold! They bought a really fun game in the shops, so they're entertained for the whole flight.

The dinosaurs head straight to the beach to warm up!

They spot some children having fun in the sea with some inflatables that look just like them and it reminds them of home back in Prehistoria.

Next stop, it's the theme park!

There are loads of rides to go on; they can't wait to get in the queue for the dinosaur rollercoaster and the big slide.

Mmm something smells good! The dinosaurs find themselves passing through a busy market with lots of lovely fresh food.

Whilst on the lookout for their next destination, the dinosaurs hear lots of splashing about and laughter – it's a pool party!

They can't wait to jump in.

The dinosaurs stumble upon a film set – and it's a film about dinosaurs!

There's a very exciting atmosphere here; the dinosaurs love the camera equipment and feel very at home on set.

These hot Hollywood dinosaurs need to cool off. There's so much to see under the sea!

The dinosaurs have had loads of fun on their adventure but they're missing home. Just as they're thinking about how to get back to Prehistoria, they spot a strange swirling blue whirlpool in the depths of the ocean. Unafraid, they swim towards it...

Whoosh! The dinosaurs come tumbling out of the swirling hole and they're back home in Prehistoria again!

What an incredible adventure.

Solutions

and extra things to find

Extra things to find:

- [ ] A lost mermaid holding a star
- [ ] A superhero
- [ ] A green alien
- [ ] A blue satellite
- [ ] A pink flying saucer

Extra things to find:

- [ ] A rocking horse
- [ ] A giant teddy bear
- [ ] A purple elephant
- [ ] A blue toy motorbike
- [ ] A trumpet

Extra things to find:

- [ ] A runner with wings
- [ ] A very hot dog
- [ ] A running diver
- [ ] A police chase
- [ ] A purple wizard's hat

Extra things to find:

- [ ] Polka-dot wellies
- [ ] An orange truck
- [ ] A camera operator
- [ ] A blue and orange flag
- [ ] A green hat

Extra things to find:

- ☐ A red top hat
- ☐ An injured player
- ☐ Someone holding a ball
- ☐ A security guard
- ☐ Two water sellers

Extra things to find:

- ☐ A giant hot dog
- ☐ Three waste bins
- ☐ A heart jumper
- ☐ A white hat
- ☐ A luggage trolley

Extra things to find:

- ☐ A red dinosaur costume
- ☐ A black dog
- ☐ Two snow dinosaurs
- ☐ A snow wall
- ☐ A skiing snowman

Extra things to find:

- ☐ A dog in a hat
- ☐ Three penguins
- ☐ A pink saucepan
- ☐ A pair of black skates
- ☐ An orange lantern

Extra things to find:

- ☐ A passenger running
- ☐ A toy plane
- ☐ A white suitcase
- ☐ A pair of red headphones
- ☐ A teddy bear

Extra things to find:

- ☐ A dolphin with a green ball
- ☐ A lighthouse
- ☐ An octopus
- ☐ Someone with orange shorts
- ☐ A surfer riding a wave

Extra things to find:

- [ ] A candyfloss stand
- [ ] A dog with a red neckerchief
- [ ] A balloon seller
- [ ] A toy elephant
- [ ] A pink horse

Extra things to find:

- [ ] Two bicycles
- [ ] Lobsters for sale
- [ ] Two honey bees
- [ ] An ice cream stand
- [ ] Cheese on a trolley

Extra things to find:

- [ ] Two lost llamas
- [ ] A unicorn inflatable
- [ ] A balloon archway
- [ ] A DJ
- [ ] A barbecue

Extra things to find:

- [ ] A rail of clothes
- [ ] A tiny dog
- [ ] A caveman
- [ ] A moving tree
- [ ] A long microphone

Extra things to find:
- [ ] A sword
- [ ] A pufferfish
- [ ] A treasure chest
- [ ] An anchor
- [ ] A whirlpool

Extra things to find:
- [ ] A pink llama
- [ ] Four curly trees
- [ ] A green Pterodactyl
- [ ] Two lost dragons
- [ ] A plant with blue flowers

The End